MOST VALUABLE PLAYERS

MVP

1

THE GOLD MEDAL MESS

MVP

Also by David A. Kelly

The Ballpark Mysteries® series

***Babe Ruth and the
Baseball Curse***

MOST VALUABLE PLAYERS
MVP

1

THE GOLD MEDAL MESS

David A. Kelly
illustrated by Scott Brundage

A STEPPING STONE BOOK™

Random House 🏠 New York

To all the wonderful teachers, librarians, parents, and kids
at the *real* Franklin Elementary School in West Newton, Massachusetts
—D.A.K.

For all the kids who stayed indoors drawing,
this is good research for what the other guys are up to.
—S.B.

Text copyright © 2016 by David A. Kelly
Cover art and interior illustrations copyright © 2016 by Scott Brundage
Photograph credits: p. 102: Pete Niesen/Shutterstock.com;
p. 103: Herbert Kratky/Shutterstock.com
All rights reserved. Published in the United States by Random House Children's Books,
a division of Penguin Random House LLC, New York.
Random House and the colophon are registered trademarks and A Stepping Stone Book
and the colophon are trademarks of Penguin Random House LLC.
Ballpark Mysteries® is a registered trademark of Upside Research, Inc.
Visit us on the Web!
SteppingStonesBooks.com
randomhousekids.com
Educators and librarians, for a variety of teaching tools, visit us at RHTeachersLibrarians.com
Library of Congress Cataloging-in-Publication Data
Names: Kelly, David A. (David Andrew), 1964– | Brundage, Scott, illustrator.
Title: The gold medal mess / David A. Kelly ; illustrated by Scott Brundage.
Description: New York : Random House Books for Young Readers, [2016] |
Series: MVP ; #1 | "A Stepping Stone Book." | Summary: "Five friends are ready for their school's
Olympics field day. But not everyone wants to play fair. Someone is trying to ruin the events!
Can the kids in the Most Valuable Player club solve the mystery, save the Olympics, and take home
the gold? Includes sports facts"— Provided by publisher.
Identifiers: LCCN 2015023503 | ISBN 978-0-553-51319-6 (paperback) |
ISBN 978-0-553-51320-2 (hardcover library binding) | ISBN 978-0-553-51321-9 (ebook)
Subjects: | CYAC: Sports—Fiction. | Olympics—Fiction. | Friendship—Fiction. | Clubs—Fiction. |
Schools—Fiction. | Mystery and detective stories. | BISAC: JUVENILE FICTION / Sports & Recreation
/ General. | JUVENILE FICTION / Mysteries & Detective Stories. | JUVENILE FICTION / School &
Education.
Classification: LCC PZ7.K2936 Go 2016 | DDC [Fic]—dc23
LC record available at http://lccn.loc.gov/2015023503
Printed in the United States of America
10 9 8 7 6 5 4 3 2 1
This book has been officially leveled by using the F&P Text Level Gradient™ Leveling System.

CONTENTS

MVP Stats

Meet the MVPs!

MAX

Great athlete—
and a great detective

ALICE

Archery ace
and animal lover

NICO

Can't wait to practice
and can't wait to play

LUKE

Loves to exercise
his funny bone

KAT

Captures the best
game-day moments
on camera

OLYMPIC TROUBLE

Max stared at the big round target on the other side of the gym. He held his bow steady and then let go of the string. The arrow sailed across the room.

THWAP! It stuck to the outer circle of the target.

"Nice shot!" said Max's best friend, Alice. She hopped up from the gym floor and straightened her shirt. It had a big picture of a dog on it. Alice loved animals. She had three dogs at home.

"Now it's my turn!" Alice said. She loaded an arrow into her bow and pulled

1

the string tight. *"Three . . . two . . . one . . . "*

SNAP! Alice let go.

THWAP! The arrow struck the center of the target. Bull's-eye!

"Way to go, Alice!" called a boy in a blue-striped shirt sitting on the bleachers. It was Max and Alice's friend Luke. He had come to watch them practice archery for the next day's annual school Olympics. It was Friday afternoon. Classes had just let out at Franklin Elementary School.

"I think you're definitely on target for a gold medal," Luke said as he stood up. "Get it? *On target*?"

Alice rolled her eyes. "Yes, Luke, I get it," she said. Luke loved to joke around. "Maybe if you were practicing like us you'd be able to win a medal, too."

"The only way I'm going to win is if they give out medals for not doing homework!" Luke said. He bounded off the bleachers. Luke could move fast when he wanted to, but he usually didn't want to. He always said that he was saving his energy for important things, like eating.

Max ran over to the target and tried to pull the arrows off, but their sticky suction-cup heads stuck tight. He leaned against the target and gave the arrows a good yank. After a few seconds, they came off with a popping sound.

Luke headed for the door. "I'm going outside to look for Kat," he said. "She's practicing for the relay event." Kat was Luke's twin sister. Even though they both had dark curly hair, they weren't identical twins.

"We'll meet you outside in a few minutes," Alice called. "We just have to stop by the office."

Luke nodded. He disappeared out the door. Alice and Max put their bows and arrows away in the corner. Then they picked up their backpacks and left the gym.

Their sneakers echoed as they walked down the hallway. All week, older kids from the nearby middle school had been helping to get ready for the next day's Olympics. The middle-school kids had planned the events. They had also made the bright blue-and-gold posters that lined the halls.

Max and Alice passed by the main entrance. A small table stood near the door. On it was a sign-in book and name tags for visitors to use when they entered the school. As they passed the table, something caught Max's eye.

He ran over, but instead of stopping in time, he skidded and bumped into the table. *SMACK!* The sign-in book and name tags went flying.

Max steadied the table and scrambled to pick up the stuff that he had knocked off. Max was one of the clumsier kids at Franklin.

"Nice job!" Alice called out. "I guess you're hoping to win the gold medal for messiest student!"

Max shook his head as he put the name tags back. "No, I saw something weird," he said. Max picked an envelope up from the floor. His eyes grew wide. "This is it! You've got to see this!"

Alice rushed over. Scrawled across the front of the envelope was a message in black ink.

BEWARE!
CANCEL YOUR OLYMPICS!

"Wow!" Alice said. "That's not good!"

"No, it isn't," Max said. "Let's go show Mrs. Doolin!"

Max and Alice raced to the main office. Mrs. Doolin was sitting at her desk. Behind her, the door to the principal's office was closed.

"What's the hurry?" she asked when Max and Alice flew into the room. "Are you done with the archery equipment?"

Alice nodded. "We put it back in the corner, just like you told us to," she said.

"What's wrong, then?" Mrs. Doolin asked. "You two look like you saw a ghost!"

Max held out the envelope. "This is the problem," he said.

Mrs. Doolin let out a little gasp. "Oh no!"

She took the envelope and opened it. A piece of paper fell out. Mrs. Doolin unfolded it. Her eyes grew wide as she read. She dropped the note on her desk and turned to call for the principal. "Mr. Hardy! Can you come here, please? There's something I need you to see."

While Mrs. Doolin was waiting for Mr. Hardy, Max and Alice leaned over to sneak a look at the letter. In the middle of the paper was a message:

YOUR OLYMPICS ARE A JOKE.
CANCEL THEM,
OR THE JOKE WILL BE ON YOU!

TOO MANY THREATS

Mr. Hardy rushed out of his office. He was wearing a crisp white shirt with a red-and-blue striped tie.

Mrs. Doolin handed him the envelope and note. Mr. Hardy read the note and a frown crossed his face. When he finished, he glanced at the warning on the envelope.

"Where'd you get this?" he asked.

Mrs. Doolin nodded toward Alice and Max. "They found it on the sign-in table," she said.

Mr. Hardy peered at Alice and

Max for a moment. Then he looked at the piece of paper again. "Hrmph," he grunted. He gave the note back to Mrs. Doolin and dropped the envelope in the trash can next to her desk. He waved his hand.

"I'll take care of this," Mr. Hardy said. "It's probably just someone playing a joke. Like the time Billy Sullivan programmed all the classroom whiteboards to display a message that read *School's canceled! Go home!* You kids don't have to worry. I'll check it out."

Mr. Hardy turned back toward his office and said, "Mrs. Doolin, can I see you for a moment?"

Mrs. Doolin glanced at Max and Alice. "Thanks for letting us know about this," she whispered. "I'm sure Mr. Hardy will check it out. I'll let you two know if we learn anything."

"Okay," Alice said.

Mrs. Doolin disappeared into Mr. Hardy's office. Max and Alice headed for the main entrance. When they reached it, Max gave the heavy metal door a good shove.

"Hey, watch it!" called a voice to their right. It was Doug, one of the kids helping to organize the Olympics. He was a middle school student now, but everyone knew him because he used to be a star athlete at Franklin.

Doug put his hand up to stop the door from hitting him and dropped the edge of the poster he was holding.

As the door closed, Max and Alice noticed an older girl named Millie hanging posters on the other side of the entrance. Nearby, other middle schoolers were spread out on the ground, painting large banners. The banners read *One World, One Team* and *Share the Olympic Spirit*. They were filled with Greek-looking letters, images of classical

columns, the Acropolis, crowns made from olive branches, and gold medals.

The door banged shut. Doug stared down at Max and Alice.

"Sorry!" Max said. He picked up the end of the poster and handed it back to Doug. Doug grabbed the top corner of the poster. He went back to sticking it to the wall with masking tape.

"It's okay," Doug said. "Just try to be more careful."

"Okay," Max said. He and Alice turned and headed down the front steps. But before they hit the last one, Max stopped short.

"Hang on," he said. "What if Mr. Hardy's wrong and that Olympic threat isn't a joke?"

Alice stopped and shrugged. "I don't know," she said. "What can we do about it?"

"We can investigate!" Max said. Max was always investigating something. His father was a police detective. Max wanted to be a scientist. He went to special camps during vacation weeks and in the summer. The previous summer he'd spent a week at a detective camp, where they learned how to dust for fingerprints and solve mysteries.

"We can start by getting that envelope. Maybe we can dust it for fingerprints or something." Max pointed to the window of Mr. Hardy's office. It was just to the left of the front door. They could see Mr. Hardy at his desk talking on the telephone. Mrs. Doolin was sitting nearby. "If we hurry we can get the envelope from the trash before they're done!"

Alice nodded. "All right, good idea," she said. "Let's go!"

They ran back up the steps and carefully slipped inside the front door. Max peeked into the main office. The room was empty, but they could hear Mr. Hardy's voice behind his closed door.

"They're still in there," Max said. "Now's our chance."

They tiptoed into the room and made straight for the trash can. Max dropped down and rummaged through the trash. He pulled up different scraps of paper until he found the threatening envelope. Just as he picked it up, they heard Mr. Hardy put down his phone.

Alice put her finger to her lips. She pointed at Mr. Hardy's door and motioned for Max to follow her. Max slipped the envelope into his back pocket as they sneaked closer. They didn't have to get very close to hear Mrs. Doolin and Mr. Hardy talking.

"Well, what did the chief of police say?" Mrs. Doolin asked. "That's the second threat we've gotten this week about the Olympics! *Now* will she do something about it?"

"She's going to send a police officer to the school for the games," Mr. Hardy said. "But I really hope we don't have any other problems."

"Why?" Mrs. Doolin asked.

"Because if we get any other threats, the chief of police said we'll have to cancel the Olympics!"

CHECK THE
BLUEPRINTS

The side door of the school flew open, and Max and Alice ran out. "They can't cancel the Olympics!" Max said. "We've got to tell the others."

Alice pointed to a big grassy field next to the school. "There they are," she said.

On the field, an oval racetrack had been marked out with wooden sticks and a rope. Luke and Kat were standing at the starting line that had been drawn on the grass with white chalk. Next to them was Nico, a tall boy with straight dark hair. He was one of Franklin's best athletes. Ms. Suraci, the school's PE teacher, stood nearby. She had a ponytail and wore a blue tracksuit with stripes on the side.

Max and Alice began to run over, but before they reached the starting line, Ms. Suraci held out her phone with the speaker on. They heard a voice say *"Three, two, one, go!"* and a loud buzzer split the air. The race had started! Luke, Nico, and Kat took off running. Kat quickly took the lead, with Nico hot on her heels.

Max and Alice stopped to cheer them on.

"Come on, Kat!" Alice yelled.

"Go, Nico!" Max shouted.

As the three rounded the far end of the racecourse, Nico pulled ahead of Kat. Kat's curly hair bounced up and down as she tried to catch up with him.

But Nico's long, tall body had an advantage. He was pumping his arms and running as fast as he could.

Max and Alice cheered them as they rounded the final corner. Ms. Suraci was standing at the finish line. Nico flew across the line first! Then Kat zoomed across. The bright purple ribbons holding back her curly hair streamed along behind her.

Luke finished last. He was panting and out of breath.

"Nico wins the gold!" Ms. Suraci called out. "Kat gets silver! And Luke wins bronze!"

Kat and Luke flopped on the ground to catch their breath, but Nico punched his fist into the air. "Yeah!" he said. "A gold medal in running would be great, but I really want to win the gold in gymnastics."

"No one else has a chance," Alice

said. "You're our top tumbler!" She gave Nico a high five.

As the clap from the high five echoed in the air, Nico dropped his hands to the ground and flipped his feet up over his head. His body arched into a circle as he turned two perfect handsprings!

Nico landed right in front of Max. "Ta-da!" he said. Nico loved to show off. His long arms and legs made him good at running, jumping, twisting, bouncing, flipping, spinning, and anything else that would make most other people queasy.

Alice and Ms. Suraci clapped. Then Ms. Suraci pretended to put medals around each of the runners' necks, just like they did at the real Olympics. When she was finished, Ms. Suraci checked her watch. "That was fun, kids," she said. "But I have to get going. I'll be rooting for you at the big race tomorrow!"

The kids waved goodbye to Ms. Suraci. She walked across the field to the teachers' parking lot behind the school. When she was safely out of earshot, Max leaned over to the group.

"Make sure you enjoy those medals," Max said. "Because you might not have a chance to win one tomorrow!"

Everyone looked at Max. "What do you mean?" Nico asked.

"We just heard the Olympics might be canceled!" Alice answered.

"Why?" Kat asked.

"Someone has been sending threatening messages to the school," Alice said. "We found a note saying the school should call off the Olympics."

"They can't do that!" Nico said. He slumped to the grass.

"Maybe we can figure out who did it," Kat said. "We should look for clues."

"That's what I was thinking. We need

to find out who's making our Olympics a mess!" Max said. "And I know where to start!"

Max always had a plan. He reached into his back pocket and pulled out the envelope. He held it so they could read the BEWARE warning.

"Alice and I snagged this from the trash can in the main office," Max said. "It's the envelope the note came in. I was going to try to dust it for fingerprints, so just hold it by the edges."

Max passed the envelope to Kat. She took it gently by the corners and turned it over to look at each side.

"Um, Max?" Kat said. "I don't think you need to dust this envelope for fingerprints."

"What do you mean?" Max asked.

Kat pointed at the flap on the back of the envelope. There, right above the sticky part, were two bright blue fingerprints!

"It looks like you've already found the fingerprints of the person who's threatening the Olympics!" Kat said.

The kids huddled around Kat to get a better look. The fingerprints seemed like a deep blue smudge, unless you looked closely.

"Let me see that," Max said. He took the envelope back from Kat and studied the fingerprints. Close up, he could see small, ridged lines. Max took out his phone and snapped a picture of the fingerprint. He zoomed in on the photo. It was easy to see a big swirl and lots of wavy lines. He showed his friends.

"Wow! Good thinking, Max," Luke said.

"Look at that radial loop," Max said, pointing to the screen. "And that second finger has a clear arch. These are great clues!"

"What if they came from Mrs. Doolin when she opened the envelope?" Luke asked. "Maybe she had ink on her hands or something."

"Good idea, but I don't think so," Alice said. "This looks like paint."

Alice used her fingernail to scratch off a small part of one of the blue fingerprints. Tiny blue flakes rubbed off.

"It wouldn't rub off if it was ink," Alice said. "Whoever wrote this note must have been using paint."

"Exactly," Max said. "So all we have to do to catch the Olympic troublemaker is find a match for these fingerprints!"

A PLAN

Early the next morning, the kids met at the jungle gym on the playground. They had agreed to meet an hour before the Olympics to search for more clues. Kat, Max, Nico, and Luke were waiting for Alice to arrive. While they waited, they took turns swinging from the monkey bars.

Nico swung from one side of the monkey bars to the other. He never seemed to sit still. He couldn't wait to put his balance beam, somersault, and vaulting practice to good use in the Olympics.

"Hey, if we catch the troublemaker, I know what we should do with him," Luke said. He was sitting on the end of the playground's slide. Given a choice between sports and sitting, Luke always sat.

Kat poked Luke in the shoulder. She was wearing yellow and green butterfly clips in her hair today. "Him or her!" she said. "We don't know if it's a boy or a girl yet."

Luke glared at Kat and then smiled. "Or a dog!" he added. "We should consider all the options."

Nico laughed. He dropped down from the last monkey bar. "If it was a dog, we would have found a paw print!" he said.

"Woof! Woof!" Luke said. He shook his head like a dog and let his tongue hang out until he started drooling.

Kat patted Luke's head. "Good dog," she said. "Now put your tongue back in your mouth!"

Luke laughed. He wiped the drool off his chin. "All right, but we can create a new Olympic event when we find the troublemaker," he said. "It'll be the Olympic dunk tank. We can get one of the big tanks where someone sits on a board above water until you hit the target with a baseball. We can have the Olympic troublemaker sit in it every day at recess. Then all the kids can take turns dunking him—or her—for the whole week!"

Max nodded and gave Luke a high five. "Great idea!" he said. "But what if we fill the dunk tank with chocolate pudding instead of water? That would be even cooler!"

"It might not be cooler, but it would be slimier," Luke said.

A few minutes later, Alice showed up on her bike. After locking it to the rack in front of the school, she joined everyone at the monkey bars.

"Let's start looking for clues," Alice said. "Luke and Kat can search inside the building. Nico, you take the playground. Max and I will check around the school. Look for anything suspicious."

While they were searching, the middle-school students started to arrive. They were all wearing bright purple T-shirts that read *Olympic Official*. The older kids were in charge of running the events. A little while later, Ms. Suraci showed up. She was wearing an official purple T-shirt, too, and was helping the middle-school kids set up the equipment for each event.

Eventually, all five kids returned to the monkey bars empty-handed. They continued to brainstorm. "Maybe the threatening note and phone call were just jokes," Luke said. "Or maybe someone like Quinn did it. He's always causing trouble."

Max nodded. "Maybe. Quinn got

called out of our class last week to go to the principal's office."

"Hey, look!" Nico said. "They just brought out the balance beams for the gymnastics event."

In the middle of the grassy field, a couple of seventh graders had set out a bunch of long wooden balance beams. They were just wide enough to walk on.

"Come on, Kat," Nico said. "Let's go practice."

Nico and Kat ran over to the balance beams. The rest of the kids followed. The boards were lined up a few feet apart for the start of the gymnastics event. Everyone picked a balance beam and tried to walk from one end to the other without falling off. Nico

was the fastest, but Kat was close behind.

Luke pretended that he was being forced to walk the plank. "Arrr! The pirates are after me!" he yelled as he teetered at the end of his balance beam. "Avast! It's too late!" Luke's arms flailed around in circles. He fell down onto the grass.

As Kat hopped off her balance beam, Luke reached out his hand. "Help me, sis!" he said. "There's sharks in these here waters! Back off, you sharks!" Luke pretended to swat at two sharks with his other hand.

Kat flicked her curly hair back. "Sorry, Luke," she said. "If you had helped me clean up the basement last weekend like I asked, I'd help you. But you didn't, so you're on your own with the sharks."

"Arrr!" Luke called. "My own sister! A rotten dog! I'm going down. . . ."

"Don't worry, Luke," Kat said. "Maybe the sharks will be as lazy as you were and won't bother to eat you!"

Over on the basketball court, the kids in the *Olympic Official* T-shirts had set up three archery targets and put bows and arrows out on tables. On the other side of the field, a middle-school kid with a backpack was setting up orange traffic cones for a running event.

At nine o'clock, students, teachers, and families began arriving. A couple of food trucks pulled up in the blue parking zone. A police officer arrived and stood watch.

While the other kids were practicing, Kat left to go to the bathroom. As she reached the top of the front steps, she noticed the posters taped around the door. She stared at one of them for a moment. Then she snapped a picture of it and raced back to the balance beams.

"Hey!" Kat said. "I just figured out

where the blue paint came from! Let me see that envelope again."

The kids gathered around Kat. Alice pulled the envelope out of her pocket and handed it to Kat. "Where did it come from?" she asked.

Kat pointed to the picture she had taken of the posters. "I don't know where the *fingerprint* came from, but the blue paint on the envelope seems to match the blue on the Olympic posters. It must have come from Mrs. Zane's classroom!"

Kat liked to do art projects, so she was good friends with Mrs. Zane, the school's art teacher. They all called her Zany for short. The kids in the school loved Mrs. Zane's class because she let them pick music to listen to. Sometimes she even let them take their art projects outside to work on.

Alice nodded. "We need to know for sure," she said.

Kat took the envelope from Alice. "I know where Mrs. Zane stores the paints," she said. "I'll go check."

Luke held up his hand and stopped Kat. "*You* have to get ready for the torch relay with Max and Nico," he said. He took the envelope from her. "I'll go check the paint. You three go win the event!"

And with that, Luke disappeared into the crowd.

THE TORCH RELAY TANGLE

At 9:30 a.m., Mr. Hardy spoke to the crowd from the front steps of the school. He was wearing a bright red, white, and blue shirt. Mr. Hardy welcomed everyone to the Olympics. Then he kicked off the first event—the torch relay.

"Every two years, runners carry a torch from Athens to the site of that year's summer or winter Olympics," Mr. Hardy said. "But our torch relay will be a little different from the ones you see on TV!"

Mr. Hardy motioned to Ms. Suraci.

She reached behind the podium and held up a toilet plunger. Its red rubber top pointed upward like a torch.

"Instead of using real flaming torches, we decided to have the students use toilet plungers!" Mr. Hardy said.

The crowd laughed and clapped. The students lined up in groups of three behind the orange cones that had been set up. Nico, Max, and Kat formed one line. Kat was in front. Alice stood off to the side, ready to cheer for them. Luke was still checking out the blue paint.

Ms. Suraci handed a plunger to the first person in each line. The kids had to hold the plunger upright in front of them. Then they had to run to the orange cones on the other side of the field and back before handing the plunger to the next person in line. The first group to have all their runners cross the line would be the winner.

Mr. Hardy moved to the white chalk starting line. He counted down.

"Five—four—three—two—one—"

BREEEEET!

Mr. Hardy blew a loud whistle to start the games.

Everyone watched Kat and the other competitors take off running while trying to hold their plungers straight up in front of them.

Kat took an early lead, but the red-headed boy next to her sped up and reached the far end of the field first. Just as he rounded the orange cone, his feet slid out from under him and he tumbled to the ground!

A few seconds later, Kat and a blond girl two lanes over started to go around their cones. And like the first kid, their feet flew out from under them and they rolled onto the ground, too! Before long, the runners from all six teams had slid out on the grass.

For a moment, nobody moved. Then Kat and the redheaded boy next to her tried to get up. But their feet went sliding out from under them again. They both flipped onto their backs. Their toilet plungers went flying!

Mr. Hardy and the teachers saw the trouble and ran over to help. But they all went tumbling down, too! Before long, the far end of the field was a tangle of arms and legs.

After a few minutes, Mr. Hardy and the teachers were able to crawl slowly away from the orange cones on their hands and knees. They motioned for the students to follow their lead. Once everyone was far enough from the cones, they could stand up normally.

"Wow! That was really slippery!" Mr. Hardy said. He called Mr. Jason, the school janitor, over to investigate. Mr. Jason crept carefully toward the slippery spot. When he got close, he kneeled down and rubbed his fingers in the grass. Then he brought them up to his nose and smelled.

Mr. Jason crawled gingerly back to Mr. Hardy. "It's oil," he said. "Like cooking oil. Somebody must have accidentally spilled it here."

"Can we wash it off?" Mr. Hardy asked. "We can't cancel the torch relay. It's the first event!"

Mr. Jason shook his head. "The oil won't wash off easily," he said. "But I have an idea. Let me get a tarp from inside the school. We can put that on the ground and then move the cones to a new spot. That way, we can start over."

"Good idea," Mr. Hardy said.

While Mr. Jason and two middle-school kids worked on moving the cones, Alice pulled Kat, Max, and Nico aside. "This wasn't an accident," she said. "Someone put the oil here on purpose to ruin our Olympics!"

Max looked around. The woods lay just beyond the edge of the racecourse. "Maybe they left some clues," he said. "Let's search the area while they're moving the cones."

The kids fanned out and explored along the edge of the nearby woods. Max and Nico checked through the shrubs on the right side. Kat and Alice looked under the long branches of the pine trees.

The adults were almost finished moving the cones when Kat spoke up. "Bingo!" she called out to the others. "I found something. Come here, quick!"

MATCHING PRINTS?

Kat lifted one of the long, bristly braches of a pine tree. Underneath sat a small pile of empty cooking oil bottles. Everyone leaned in to take a closer look. Kat picked one up. The clear bottle was empty. It had a shiny gold label with a big red heart on it. She took a picture of it.

"Someone probably emptied these on the grass and ditched the empty bottles here!" she said.

"Whoever did it must have done it after the orange cones were in place.

Otherwise, the kids setting up would have fallen, too!" Alice said.

TWEEEEEET!

Mr. Hardy sounded his whistle. "We are going to restart the torch relay," he called. "Please line up with your teams again."

Kat dropped the bottle back into the pile. "Let's go," she said. "We can figure this out after the race."

A few minutes later, the teams had regrouped at a new starting point. The orange cones had been moved farther down the field. The kids lined up with their plungers.

BREEEET!

Mr. Hardy blew his whistle. The race was on!

"Come on, Kat!" Alice shouted.

Kat raced down the field with the plunger held up high. This time, she didn't slip going around the orange cone. But when she handed the plunger to Max, two of the other teams were already ahead. The crowd cheered wildly as the second set of runners rounded the cones. After making it back, Max quickly handed the plunger to Nico. He took off like a shot.

It wasn't enough to catch up to the

other teams, though. Before Nico had
made it halfway back from the orange
cone, three other teams had already
crossed the finish line! That meant no
medal for Kat, Max, and Nico.

"I can't believe we lost!" Nico said.
"If only the first race wasn't messed up.
Kat was in second place before everyone slipped in the oil. We could have
won if the race wasn't called!"

"At least you still have the gymnastics event," Max said. "You're a cinch to win that!"

Just then, Alice spotted Luke. She waved him over. When he finally made it through the crowd, he pulled out a piece of paper with a big splotch of blue painted in the center. He held the envelope with the fingerprint on it next to the splotch of paint.

"Wow!" Max said.

"The paint matches exactly!" Luke said. "It took me a while because I had to let the paint dry."

"That's a perfect match!" Alice said. She took the envelope back from Luke and slipped it into her pocket. "Now we just need to find out who's been using that paint!"

"It's probably the same person who drizzled all the oil by the orange cones," Max said. He told Luke about the torch relay tangle. Kat showed him the picture of the empty oil bottles.

"What if it's one of the middle-school kids?" Luke asked. "They've been using the blue paint for the posters. Maybe we should check them out?"

"Good idea," Kat said.

But when they looked around the field, there were a lot of middle-school kids there. Everywhere they looked, helpers in purple T-shirts were setting up the events, running the activity stands, or handing out food.

"There are too many of them," Nico said.

"What if we ask Mrs. Zane?" Kat said. "Maybe someone else has been using blue paint."

"Okay," Max said. "Let's spread out and look. If anyone finds her, just give a whistle."

The kids wound their way through families enjoying popcorn and other snacks and passed tables filled with activities like face painting.

A few minutes later, Nico gave four long whistles from the edge of the crowd. He had found Mrs. Zane near a snack table stocked with orange slices, popcorn, granola bars, and raisins. The kids ran over.

Kat stepped forward. "Mrs. Zane,"

she said, "we have a question for you."

"Oh, hi, Kat," Mrs. Zane said. "What's my favorite artist up to now? Have you taken any good photos today?"

Kat blushed. "I'm working on it," she said. "But we wanted to show you something we found."

Alice pulled out the envelope and showed Mrs. Zane the blue fingerprints. Kat told her they thought the blue paint was the key to finding the Olympic troublemaker. "The fingerprints match the blue paint in the art room," Kat said. "Has anyone else been using it lately?"

Mrs. Zane thought for a moment. "Well," she said, "the middle-school students have been using my paints to make all those signs and banners."

Luke looked around the field at the kids in the purple shirts. "We thought of that," he said. "But we can't investigate all of them. There are too many."

Mrs. Zane nodded. "Yes, that could

be a problem," she said. Mrs. Zane tapped her fingers on the table. "But now that I'm thinking about it, I gave Quinn some blue paint yesterday for a project he's doing for the principal."

"I'll bet that's it!" Max said. He looked around at the crowd. It seemed like it had grown even bigger in the last few minutes. "Now we just need to find Quinn."

"Actually, that might be easy," Mrs. Zane said. "I saw him this morning when I parked my car. He's working in the storage garage." The storage garage was in the back of the school, near the teachers' parking lot.

"Thanks," Kat said to Mrs. Zane.

"You're welcome," Mrs. Zane said as she turned to go. "Good luck figuring out your mystery!"

"See, I told you it might be Quinn!" Luke said to Alice after Mrs. Zane had left.

BREEEET!

Mr. Hardy's whistle blew again. It was time for the next event. "The tug-of-war will be starting in fifteen minutes!" he called out.

Luke tapped Max and Alice on their shoulders. "That's us!" he said. Max, Alice, and Luke were on a tug-of-war team together. "We should get ready for the event!"

Alice bit her lip. "Mr. Hardy said fifteen minutes," she said. "That's enough time for me and Max to find Quinn. You three can check the tug-of-war for any problems. We'll check the other events when the tug-of-war is over."

"Got it!" Nico said. He, Kat, and Luke took off toward the tug-of-war event.

Alice and Max walked into the storage garage. A boy with curly red hair was using a piece of sandpaper to smooth the shelves of a wooden bookcase.

"Hi, Quinn," Max said. "Mrs. Zane told us you were back here working on a project."

Quinn patted the top of the bookcase. "Yup," he said. "Mr. Hardy told me that if I fixed up a couple of old bookcases, I won't have to pay the school

back for the window I broke last week."
Quinn pointed to a second bookcase behind him. It was already finished and
painted bright blue.

"Sounds like a good deal," Alice said.

"Mrs. Zane also said you were using
some of her blue paint," Max said.

Quinn nudged a paint bucket on the
floor with his foot. "Yeah, so what?" he
asked. "I'm going to start painting this
bookcase in a little while."

Alice took out the envelope with
the fingerprints on it. She held it up so
Quinn could read the BEWARE message
on its front. "Do you know anything
about this?" she asked. "We found it on
the sign-in table."

Quinn put down the sandpaper and
shrugged. "Nope," he said. "I've never
seen it before."

"There was a note inside threatening
to ruin our Olympics," Max said.

Alice flipped the envelope over. She pointed to the two blue fingerprints on the back. Then she looked at Quinn.

"You think those are mine?" Quinn asked.

"Maybe," Max said.

"They're not," Quinn said.

"Prove it!" Alice said.

Quinn rolled his eyes. "Sure," he said. "But you're not going to like the answer. I've never seen that before."

Alice flipped the sandpaper over so the rough side was down and the paper back was facing up. "Put a little paint on your fingers and press them on this sandpaper," she said.

Quinn dipped the tips of the fingers on his right hand into the paint and pressed them down on the sandpaper. When he lifted them up, there were five blue fingerprints left behind.

Max pulled out his phone and

flipped through his pictures until the phone displayed the one he had taken of the fingerprints on the envelope. The three leaned over to compare the fresh prints to Max's phone.

After a minute, Max straightened up. Quinn smiled.

The fingerprints were completely different!

A BIG BREAK

"I really thought it was going to be Quinn," Max said after they had left the storage garage.

"I know," Alice said. "But those fingerprints weren't even close."

They turned the corner of the building and headed back to the field. All around them, students, parents, and teachers were enjoying the Olympics. There were long lines in front of the Cheezy Wheezy grilled cheese truck and the Green Pirate juice and salad truck in the blue zone. Near the side of the school, Ms. Suraci was running a Hula-Hoop workout for kids and parents.

Just as they made it back to the middle of the field, Kat ran up to them. "We checked out the tug-of-war, but it's fine," she said. "Luke and Nico will meet us there in a few minutes. Nico wanted to try the spicy sweet potato sticks at the snack table." In addition to being the best athlete, Nico was the school's most adventurous eater. He'd try anything!

"Great!" Alice said. "We found Quinn, but he's definitely not our guy. The fingerprints didn't match." Alice checked the time. "Hey, we can still try the archery stuff before the tug-of-war."

Alice, Max, and Kat pushed through the crowds to the archery area. Three large, round targets were set up on the right side of the basketball court. A line of blue tape stretched across the ground on the other side. Alice headed straight for the bows and arrows on a nearby table.

"I can't wait for archery," Alice said. "I practiced all week for it."

"There's no way anyone will beat you," Kat said. "You're the best!"

Alice picked up a bow and arrow from the table. She focused on the target.

SNAP!

Alice let go of the bowstring. The

arrow flew straight to the target across the basketball court.

THWAP!

"Wow!" Max cried. "You got a bull's-eye on your first try! Way to go!"

Alice smiled and gave Max a high five. She placed the bow back on the table and looked at the other bows and arrows. Kat ran over to the target. She grabbed hold of the arrow and pulled. The suction cup on its tip made a *pop* sound when she pulled it off the target.

Kat brought it back to the table. "There's nothing wrong with the targets," she said.

"And there's nothing wrong here," Alice said. "I guess we're lucky that the Olympic troublemaker doesn't care about archery!"

Max looked over to the field. "We should go. It looks like the tug-of-war is about to start," he said.

Max, Alice, and Kat ran back through the crowd to the tug-of-war event. They arrived just before it started and found Nico and Luke, who were finishing up their spicy sweet potato sticks.

For the tug-of-war, someone had painted a bright blue line across the grass. A long rope stretched across the line. There was a red triangle flag in the middle, pointing down at the line. It made it easier to see who was winning or losing.

Max, Alice, and Luke lined up with three other teammates on the left side of the rope. They faced six students on the other side. Max took a position on the rope closest to the flag. Luke was at the end of the rope, acting as anchor for their team. Alice was in the middle. The kids all gripped the rope tightly. The first team to be pulled across the blue line would lose.

Kat wormed her way up to the

front of the crowd so she could take some pictures. Nico stood behind her to cheer.

Mr. Hardy blew his whistle loudly. *BREEEET!*

Both teams pulled with all their might. At first, the rope moved toward Max, Alice, and Luke's side. Kat started snapping pictures right away.

Nico yelled and clapped. "Come on, Luke!

You've got it!" he called. "Just keep pulling!"

But a minute later, the rope moved in the opposite direction. Max was pulled closer and closer to the blue line on the ground. He dug his feet in, but they kept slipping forward. "We're losing!" he yelled.

Luke called from the back, "On the count of three, everyone pull hard. One, two, *three!*"

Luke's team gave a huge tug on the

rope. The other team was yanked forward.

"It's working!" Max cried. "It's working!"

But before they could drag the other team across the line to win, there was a sudden lurch. Both teams seemed to shudder and slip.

SNAP!

The tug-of-war rope broke in half!

A MATCHING PAIR

Parents and teachers gasped as both teams tumbled backward! The kids looked like dominoes as they fell to the ground.

BREEEET! BREEEET!

Mr. Hardy blew his whistle. "Quiet, everyone! Step back!" he barked. The kids scrambled to stand up.

Kat snapped picture after picture.

Mr. Hardy stepped forward. He checked to make sure that all the kids were okay. Once he determined that, he glanced at his watch.

"Don't worry! I'll have Mr. Jason look for another rope. We'll redo the tug-of-war a little later," he said. "For now, we can get ready for the gymnastics event. We'll start that in ten minutes. And we'll do archery after that."

As the crowd moved away, Nico and Kat drifted over to the tug-of-war rope. Max, Alice, and Luke were looking at each side of the rope's broken ends.

"Hey, look! This rope didn't just break," Max said. He showed them the two ends of the rope. Strands of fiber frizzed out from both sides. But about half of the strands weren't frizzy. Instead, they had been cut!

Alice held up the red flag lying on the ground. It had been hanging down from the middle of the rope. "The Olympic troublemaker must have used a knife or scissors to cut the rope halfway through so it would break during the event," she said. "Then he or she covered the cut with this flag so it would look normal!"

"That's why we didn't see any problems when we checked the rope!" Kat said. "Tricky!"

As Max and Alice studied the rope, Kat pulled out her camera. "Look, I got some pictures just as the rope snapped!" she said. "Here are Max and Alice falling backward!"

The kids leaned in to look at the pictures. But as Kat swiped through them, Alice said, "Stop! What's that?" She pointed to one of the kids in the background. It was a middle schooler in a purple T-shirt.

"That's Doug," Max said. "He set the record for winning the most medals at last year's Olympics. He won two gold medals, two silver medals, and one bronze."

"I know who Doug is," Alice said. Over Kat's shoulder, Alice swiped back and forth through the pictures. "But look at all these pictures. When the rope breaks, Doug is smiling and laughing. Everyone else looks serious or surprised!"

"You're right," Kat said. As Alice moved back and forth between the pictures, Doug really stood out. He looked just like one of the crowd until the rope broke. Then he had a wide smile at the same time that everyone else was gasping!

"Why is he doing that?" Kat asked. "It almost looks like he thinks it's funny!"

"Maybe he does," Alice said.

"What do you mean?" Kat asked.

"Maybe he thinks it's funny because he's the one who cut the rope!" Alice said.

"Why would he do that?" Nico asked.

"That's easy," Alice said. "Max just said he won the most medals last year. What if he's sabotaging our Olympics so no one can beat his record?"

Alice pointed across the field to the oily spot near the orange cones. "Maybe Doug was helping to set up the events. He could have poured the oil near the orange cones *after* they were put out. He probably did it when the other kids were busy with another event."

"If Doug's the one doing it," Mike said, "we need to find him before he does something else!"

Everyone nodded. They looked around the field. But it was hard to find anyone with all the people moving around.

Nico pointed to the front of the school. "Hey, let's go to the steps," he said. "It'll be easier to spot Doug from up there."

"Good idea," Kat said. The kids ran over to the steps and bounded up to the top. As they looked for Doug, Alice glanced at the posters taped to the front of the school. The posters were filled with blue-and-gold letters and pictures of ancient Rome. Alice spotted one that had the words *Light the Fire Within* in blue letters outlined in gold. Something in the top right corner caught her eye.

"Hey, Max," she said. "Wasn't this the poster that Doug was hanging up yesterday?"

Max looked at it. "Yeah, that's the one," he said. The poster had a big picture of the Parthenon on it.

"That's what I thought," Alice said. "Check this out." She pointed to the top right corner of the poster. "That's where Doug grabbed the poster when he was putting it back up after you knocked it down," she said. "The paint on it must have been wet. Look what's there."

There were three blue fingerprints along the top of the poster!

Max fumbled for his back pocket. Finally, he took out his phone. He pulled up the photo he had taken of the blue fingerprints on the envelope and held it against the poster.

Alice and the others leaned in.

They matched exactly!

A SLIPPERY TARGET

"Now we've got proof that Doug is the Olympic troublemaker!" Max said. "All we have to do is find him before he ruins another event!"

The kids continued to scan the fields for any sign of Doug. But all they saw were kids, parents, and teachers standing in line for one of the food trucks or trying one of the games of skill set up in the center of the field. Nico and Luke studied the left side of the field, while Max, Alice, and Kat searched the right side.

As they looked, Nico kept glancing over to the balance beams. "Well, if he's not out here, he can't be ruining an event," Nico finally said. "Maybe we should get back to the Olympics. I don't want to miss the gymnastics event. We can look for Doug again after."

"I guess," Alice said. "We're not having any luck now."

The group walked down the front steps and over to the field. Nico approached one of the officials, who assigned him a balance beam to use.

The gymnastics competition was like an obstacle course. The competitors had to walk the entire length of their balance beam without falling off. If the competitor fell off, he or she would have to start over again. After finishing the balance beam, the competitors had to do somersaults or cartwheels until they reached a turnaround line painted on the field.

To complete the event, the kids had to jump or vault over big piles of sandbags on their way back to the starting line.

BLEEEET! BLEEEET!

Mr. Hardy blew his whistle. The gymnastics event was about to start! Nico and five other kids lined up at the end of the beams. Mr. Hardy explained the rules and then counted down.

"Five–four–three–two–one!" Mr. Hardy called.

BREEEET!

All six kids started walking down the balance beams. The boy next to Nico fell off after two steps and started over. The tall girl at the far end fell off after four, and then ran back to the starting point.

"Go, Nico! Go!" Kat and Luke shouted.

Max and Alice clapped and whooped loudly when Nico made it to the end of the balance beam without falling off. So far, he was tied for first place with a girl

named Jen. Nico and Jen both bounded off the beams at the same time and ran to a white chalk line in the grass. A short boy named Don was just behind both of them in third place.

"Way to go, Nico!" Alice shouted.

When the kids reached the white line, all three tipped forward and started doing one somersault after another. A student in a purple Olympic T-shirt counted everyone's somersaults to make sure they all did at least five and then kept doing them until they reached the turnaround line.

Nico finished his first! Don and Jen were still on their fourth somersault.

"You've got it, Nico!" Kat screamed. "Go! Go! Go!"

When Nico crossed the turnaround line painted on the grass, he jumped up. Then he did a U-turn and started to run back to the starting line. To win the gold medal, all he had to do was vault over a pile of sandbags and make it to the finish line first.

"Go, Nico!" Max yelled. He, Alice, Luke, and Kat cheered like crazy! It was the friends' first real chance to win a medal!

Back behind Nico, Jen and Don finished their somersaults and then popped up off the ground. They tried to catch up with Nico, but it was going to be hard.

Before Nico reached the sandbags, he held up his hands and stopped running! Instead of finishing the race, he ducked to the side of the course and disappeared into the crowd. Mr. Hardy, who was also watching, pointed to where Nico had been, blew his whistle, and shouted "Disqualified!"

Max, Alice, Kat, and Luke couldn't believe it!

Jen and Don crossed the finish line for the gold and silver gymnastics medals! A fourth grader named Sam came in third for a bronze medal.

"What just happened?" Max said. "Did Nico go nuts?"

Luke shook his head like he couldn't believe it. "He was just about to win!" he said.

The crowd surged around Jen, Don, and Sam to congratulate them. Max, Alice, Luke, and Kat stood there, stunned, until Max finally spotted Nico by the drinking fountain.

"There he is!" Max said. He took off in a run, followed by the others. Seconds later, they skidded to a halt in front of the fountain. Nico was staring at the corner of the basketball court.

"Nico, are you okay?" Alice asked. "What just happened? You could have won a gold medal!"

Nico glanced at the group and then looked back toward the basketball court. "I *know* I could have," he said. "That's one of the reasons why I stopped. Once I knew I could win the gold medal if I wanted to, it didn't matter anymore."

Max jumped up and down. "Are you crazy?" he yelped. "I'd love to win a gold medal!"

"I would, too," Nico said. "But I'd rather catch Doug! That's the real reason I dropped out. On my way back to the finish line, I spotted Doug on the basketball court. I didn't want to risk losing him! Look—he's right over there!"

The kids glanced over at the court.

Nico was right. Doug was standing near the archery equipment! They watched as he straightened up the bows and arrows and counted them. But after taking a quick look around, Doug slipped the backpack off his shoulder and dropped it on the ground. He unzipped it and reached in with both hands. He seemed to be fumbling with something inside the bag. When he stood up, he had a white cloth in his hand. He glanced around again and then started picking up one arrow after another.

"What's he doing?" Alice asked.

Max strained to see. "I don't know," he said, "but I think he's doing something to the tips of the arrows! I wonder what's in the bag."

As they watched, Doug squatted down and put the cloth back into the backpack for a moment. Then he pulled it out and continued picking up the arrows one by one.

"What is he doing to those arrows?" Alice asked. "We need to find out what's in the bag."

"Hey!" Max said. "I've got an idea. But I'll need some volunteers."

Kat and Luke quickly raised their hands.

Max tapped Nico on his shoulder. "Hey, I'll need you, too," Max said. "You in?"

Nico nodded. "I'm in!" he said.

Max gathered them into a huddle and whispered some instructions. A minute later, they broke up. Kat, Nico, and Luke ran over to the climbing structure on the empty playground just beyond the basketball court.

"What's going on?" Alice asked. "I thought you were going to get them to help us catch Doug!"

Max smiled. "I did," he said. "Just wait here and watch. Then follow me when I run!"

Alice raised an eyebrow but did what Max said.

From the playground, Kat looked back at Max. Max raised his right hand and gave her a thumbs-up. As soon as he did that, Kat went into the middle of the climbing structure and dropped down into the wood chips on the ground. Then she grabbed her ankle and started crying!

"What's going on?" Alice asked. "How's this going to help?"

"Just watch," Max said.

As soon as Kat started crying, Nico and Luke ran over to Doug on the basketball court. They tugged on the sleeve of his purple T-shirt and pointed to Kat on the ground. Reluctantly, Doug put down his white cloth and ran back to the climbing structure with Nico and Luke.

"Now!" Max said. He took off like a flash for the basketball court. Alice ran along behind him. Max headed straight for the bows and arrows. Alice skidded to a stop next to him. Max picked up the rag and touched it. He pulled his fingers away and rubbed them together.

"It's oil!" Max said. "Doug's putting something slippery on the tips of the arrows so they won't stick to the targets!"

Alice looked over her shoulder at the climbing structure. Nico and Luke were keeping Doug busy trying to help Kat.

Alice dropped to her knees. She pulled open the top of Doug's backpack. Then she gasped. "Jackpot!" she said.

"What's in there?" he asked.

Before Max could get a look at what was in the backpack, Alice grabbed its bottom and flipped it upside down! A half-full bottle of cooking oil bounced on the ground. It had the same label as the ones they had found under the tree branch. It was followed by a large pair of scissors and a spool of clear fishing line.

Alice smiled. "I think we've caught the person who's turning our Olympics into a mess!"

GOLD MEDAL MVPs

Alice glanced over at the climbing structure. Doug was still trying to help Kat stand up. Alice scooped up all the items and slipped them into the backpack.

"Quick, Max," Alice said. "Go get Mr. Hardy! I'll stay here and guard the bag."

Max nodded and ran off through the crowd. Alice stood up and used her heel to push the bag under the table. When she turned back to check on Doug, her eyes widened. Doug was running straight for her!

Alice tried to look busy by straightening up the arrows. But a few seconds later, Doug stopped right beside her. He pulled all the arrows away from her.

"Sorry, but this event isn't set up yet," he said. "I'm still working on it."

He bent over and tried to grab his backpack from under the table, but Alice stepped sideways and blocked him from reaching it.

"Hey! What are you doing?" Doug asked. "That's my backpack!"

"I know," Alice said. "That's why we're going to have Mr. Hardy take a look inside it. And then maybe he'll know who's been making all the trouble at our Olympics!"

"Wh-wh-what do you mean?" Doug stammered. "Give it to me!"

Doug tried to grab the backpack again, but Alice nudged it farther under the table with her feet.

"Cut it out!" Doug said. He dropped to his hands and knees and crawled under the table. He grabbed the backpack and scurried out from under the table. Doug stood up, only to find Mr. Hardy standing in front of him.

"Ah, Doug! How nice of you to pick up your backpack for us," Mr. Hardy said. He held out his hand and took hold of one of the backpack straps. "Max told me I might want to see what's inside."

Doug slowly let go of the bag.

Mr. Hardy unzipped the main compartment. He pulled out the half-full bottle of cooking oil, the fishing line, and the scissors. "Hmmmmmm." Mr. Hardy put the items back in and zipped the backpack shut. "You're coming with me, Doug. We'll go to the office to call your parents."

Doug's shoulders dropped. He hung his head and followed Mr. Hardy.

Max, Alice, Luke, Nico, and Kat were standing near the water fountain when Mr. Hardy found them.

"There you are," Mr. Hardy said. "Thank you so much for alerting me to Doug's bag of tricks. It looks like he wanted to mess up the Olympics. The police officer is questioning Doug now."

"But why was Doug trying to ruin our games?" Kat asked.

Mr. Hardy shook his head. "It was just like Max thought. Doug didn't want anyone to win more medals than he did," he said. "So he has been plotting ways to mess up our Olympics. He was hoping they'd be canceled."

The kids nodded.

"I guess you could say he's a sore winner," Alice said.

Mr. Hardy chuckled. "I'd say so," he said. "Since Doug was helping to set up the events, he was able to think up ways to disrupt them. If you hadn't stopped him, he was going to ruin the water balloon race and the rest of the events."

"Wow!" said Luke.

"But we're lucky. You kids caught

him, so he didn't finish setting any other traps," Mr. Hardy said. "Do you know what that means?"

Max glanced at Luke, who looked at Alice. Kat and Nico shrugged.

"No, what?" Max asked.

"It means you saved the Olympics!" Mr. Hardy said. "Now we can continue them and no one will get hurt! Great job!"

Mr. Hardy gave each of the kids a high five. "Come on," he said. "We have to get the games started again."

They walked back with him to the tug-of-war area. Mr. Jason had found another rope and was testing it out to make sure it was safe. As they waited for the games to resume, news of Doug's traps and Alice, Max, Kat, Luke, and Nico's efforts to catch him spread quickly through the crowd.

And just like Mr. Hardy said, the rest of the events went smoothly. Even though they tried hard, Max, Alice, and Luke's team lost the second tug-of-war match. Luke and Kat almost won the water balloon toss, but Luke dropped the balloon and they were disqualified. Unfortunately, Alice and Max weren't able to compete for a medal in archery. That event had to be canceled because the arrows were still too slippery, even after Doug's oil had been rubbed off.

When all the events were finished, everyone gathered in the Franklin School cafeteria. The stage at the far end had been set up with banners. Mr. Hardy gave out gold, silver, and bronze medals for all the different events. He called up the winners in groups of threes.

Alice, Max, Luke, Nico, and Kat sat together at one of the tables. Alice fidgeted and scuffed the ground with her sneaker as she watched one group of winners after another get their medals.

"I really wanted to win a medal for archery," Alice said to Max. "I might have won gold!"

Max nodded. "You would have!" he said. Then he shrugged. "But at least we were able to capture Doug. I guess that way at least everyone *else* got to enjoy the Olympics."

When Mr. Hardy finished giving out

the medals, the crowd clapped for all the winners. People were about to leave when Mr. Hardy stepped back up to the microphone.

"If you can hold on for just another moment, we saved something special for the end," he said. "I'd like to ask Alice, Max, Luke, Kat, and Nico to come up to the stage."

Alice and Max had big smiles on their faces. They scrambled up the stairs with Nico, Luke, and Kat and crossed the stage to Mr. Hardy.

As the kids approached, Mr. Hardy announced, "I think by now everyone has heard about the problems with some of our events this morning. I just wanted you all to see the kids who helped catch our Olympic troublemaker."

Mr. Hardy stepped back and swept his hands in the direction of the five of them. The crowd clapped. When the clapping died down, Mr. Hardy moved back up to the microphone.

"I also wanted to apologize to Max and Alice. I should have taken the threatening note they found more seriously," he said. "But luckily, *they* didn't listen to *me* when I said the note was nothing to worry about!"

Everyone laughed.

"Max and Alice and their friends were smart enough to put the clues together and find the troublemaker," Mr. Hardy said. "In recognition for Alice, Max, Luke, Kat, and Nico's terrific work today in saving the Olympics, I'm awarding each of them the first-ever Franklin School Most Valuable Player medals! They're the MVPs of our Olympics!"

Mr. Hardy walked down the line and slipped a gold medal on a red, white, and blue ribbon over each kid's head.

Max, Alice, Nico, Kat, and Luke's faces erupted into broad smiles. The crowd cheered loudly. After a minute, the noise died down and everyone filed out of the cafeteria. But Alice pulled the others to a huddle on the side of the stage.

She held up her Most Valuable Player medal. "It's really nice that we got the MVP medals," she said. "But I think the

best thing about today wasn't just saving the Olympics. It was how we worked together. I think we should form a club. The MVP Club!"

Max nodded. "That's a great idea," he said. "All in favor of joining the MVP Club raise your hand."

Five hands went up.

"Motion passed," Alice said. "It's official. We're now the Franklin School MVP Club."

"Yahoo!" Max yelled. "Group high five, everyone! On the count of three!"

"One, two, three!" Max called out. All at once, five hands shot up to the center of the circle for a group high five. *SLAP!*

And with that, the Franklin School MVP Club headed home.

MVP
Stats

The Olympics

OLYMPIC RINGS. The five Olympic rings represent different regions of the world: Africa, America, Asia, Europe, and Oceania.

NAKED. The original Olympics were held in Greece in 776 BC. The best athletes came from all over Greece to compete in events that ranged from racing to javelin throwing, much like today's Olympics. But one big thing was different back then: the athletes all competed *without their clothes on!* It was thought that they would perform better that way.

ONE-HIT WONDER. Some sports have been in the Olympics only once. Croquet was only an Olympic sport once, in 1900.

EVENTS. The Olympics happen every two years, alternating between winter and summer. Many events stay the same (there has always been a running race). But over time, the Olympic committee drops unpopular sports and adds new ones. Gymnastics has been in all mod-

ern summer Olympics. Snowboarding was added at the 1998 Winter Games.

YOUNGEST OLYMPIAN. The youngest person to win a medal in modern times was Dimitrios Loundras. Dimitrios came from Greece. He was a gymnast (like Nico) in the 1896 Athens Olympics, and he was only ten years old!

GOLD MEDALS AREN'T GOLD. Back in late 1800s and early 1900s, the Olympic gold medals were made of gold. Today's gold medals are mostly made of silver, but they are coated with a layer of gold. Silver and bronze medals are made of silver and bronze.

Turn the page for
a sneak peek at

"Over here!" Kat called as she ran toward the other team's goal. "I can do it!"

There were only seconds left in the soccer game. The Franklin Elementary School girls were playing the boys. The game was tied 1–1.

Kat's best friend Alice lofted a pass to her. Kat trapped the ball with her foot. She turned for the shot and blasted it. Kat's teammates screamed as the ball sliced through the air toward the goal!

But the ball hit the post and bounced over the top of the net. No goal! The gym teacher's whistle blew. Game over. It was a tie.

The boys' team cheered! A tie was better than losing. The girls drifted off the field with shoulders drooped. They would have won if Kat's shot had gone in.

Alice skidded to a stop beside Kat.

Alice was athletic and lucky. Even when she missed a shot or messed up a pass, she usually scored the next goal or soon made a nice assist.

"Aw! I was so close!" Kat cried. She dropped down to the grass and pulled a bright blue hair tie from her hair. Black curls tumbled around her neck.

"Good try," Alice said. "Just a bit to the right and you would have had it."

"I keep missing those shots!" Kat said. "I've got to find a way to get better before the big game in two weeks."

Each year, the girls' team played the Wilton Warriors. Lots of people came to watch and cheer their team on. The Warriors usually won, but Franklin's team had been practicing hard. They really wanted to win this year.

Kat's twin brother, Luke, walked up next to her. He patted her on the shoulder.

"Nice try, sis," Luke said. "But thanks for missing that goal!"

Kat bit her lip. She grabbed a handful of grass and tossed it up at Luke. As he swatted it away, Kat swung her arm playfully behind his legs and knocked into the back of his knees. He flailed back and forth for a moment and then dropped to the ground.

Kat smiled. "Oh, sorry!" she said. "I

was just stretching. How many goals did *you* score?"

Luke held his hands up. "None," he admitted. "But maybe you *should* work on your shooting."

Kat flopped on her back and looked up at the sky. "I have been!" she said. "You've seen me practicing after dinner. What more can I do?"

"I don't know, but you need to find a way to get better before Alex Akers comes for the big game," Luke said.

Luke and Kat's mom was friends with Alex Akers, the women's soccer star. They had played soccer together in college. She was coming to stay with them in two weeks to watch Kat's big game. Alex was on the best team in women's soccer, the Breakers. She had won the Player of the Year award for the last three years.

Alice tapped Kat on the knee. "Why

don't you ask Alex to help you work on your shooting?" she asked. "Maybe she'd give you some tips."

Kat sat up. "That's a great idea!" she said. A big smile spread across her face. She jumped up and did a couple of air kicks. "Zap! Zam! Another score by Alex Akers!" She kicked again. "And one by Kat!"

"Hey, maybe I can get some pointers, too!" Luke said.

"No!" Kat said. "You don't always have to do everything that *I* do. Your team isn't playing in the big game. If you go near her, I'll give *you* a shot!"

"Oh yeah?" Luke asked. He hitched his shoulders back and turned to face Kat. "Just try to stop me. . . ."

Alice laughed and jumped in between them. "Hey, maybe she'll have time to give you *both* some soccer tips," she said. Alice tugged Kat's arm. "We need to get over to the field house for our ride."

Alice, Luke, and Kat gathered their things and ran to catch up with their friends. Max and Nico were standing in front of the field house at the corner of the soccer field. The field house was an old two-story building. It had been used for summer camps and storing athletic equipment, but the town closed it a few years ago because it needed repairing.

"Hey, Alice, when's your dad getting here?" Max said. He was kicking a soccer ball against the side of the field house.

"About ten minutes," Alice said.

Just then, a kid from the boys' soccer team walked by with his father, who was also the boys' soccer coach. They were headed to their car.

"Hey, Danny," Nico said. "Nice goal in today's game!"

Danny gave a thumbs-up. "Thanks,"

he said. "But I'm still not as good as you, Nico!" Nico was one of the best athletes in the school.

"Hey, Alice and Kat, good game!" Danny's father, Mr. Danforth, said. He was a tall man with short black hair. Even when he was coaching, he always wore a suit and tie.

Danny got into the car with his father, and they drove away.

"Isn't Mr. Danforth trying to tear down the field house?" Alice asked.

Kat nodded. "The town doesn't have enough money to fix it, and Mr. Danforth wants to build an office building," Kat said. "My mom's in a group trying to save it."

Nico looked up at the front of the building. It needed a good painting, and half the shutters were missing. "It's too bad," he said.

While they waited for Alice's father,

Max and Nico took turns trying to hit a spot on the wall with the soccer ball. Nico was definitely a better shot, but Max was having fun kicking the ball as hard as he could.

A few minutes later, the kids heard a door slam shut across the street. An older man with a hat had just left his house to walk his dog.

"It's Mr. Jennings," Alice said. "Maybe he'll come over here with Sammy."

"Mr. Jennings is the one who's always mean to kids," Max said.

"I know," Alice said. "But his dog, Sammy, is nice. I'm going to see if I can pet him."

Alice loved all types of animals. Even though she had three dogs at home, she was always excited to see other dogs or cats. When Mr. Jennings reached the sidewalk in front of the field house, Alice ran over to pet

Sammy. She returned a few minutes later when Mr. Jennings continued on his walk.

"Hey, Alice, watch this!" Max called out as she came back. He trapped the soccer ball and pulled his leg back to kick as hard as he could.

WHAP!

Max whacked the ball hard with his foot. But instead of kicking it straight on, he caught the edge of the ball and it sliced to the right.

"Oh no!" Max called out. "Stop it!"

But it was too late.

CRASH!

The ball smashed right through the front window of the field house!

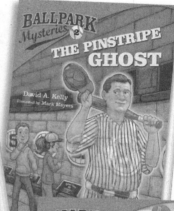

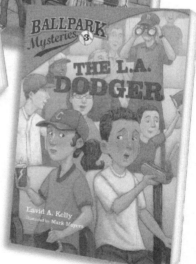

Get ready for more baseball adventure!

Did Babe Ruth curse the Boston Red Sox when he moved to the New York Yankees?

Available now!